THE ADVENTURES OF
SUKIE, TRISTAN AND JEREMY JAY

PAM SWAIN

DEDICATION

To my grandsons, Ethan, Justin, Noah and Max. You are my inspirations.

CONTENTS

SUKIE, TRISTAN AND JEREMY JAY

Sukie touched the little box in her pocket and smiled. She thought of the reaction it would get when she let the spider out in her brother Tristan's bed. He had been more nasty and mean to her than usual lately, and she was determined to get her own back. She loved bugs and nature and when she saw the huge hairy spider she gently put it into a matchbox and put holes in the top to keep it alive. Tristan hated bugs and was scared of spiders in particular but she felt if she really frightened him maybe he would leave her alone once and for all.

 She was three years younger than Tristan and he seemed to think she was just there for his amusement. Once he had taken her into their cloakroom, told her to stand on her rocking horse that he had pushed up against the wall where the coat pegs were and told her to put her hands up in the air. Then he tied her thumbs to the coat hooks and took the rocking horse away. As she dangled from the hooks by her thumbs she promised herself that she wouldn't trust him again.

Sukie had long brown hair that flowed down over her shoulders. It was nearly always in a braid or plaits. She had green eyes and a few freckles on her nose. Jeremy Jay was Sukie's most prized possession. He was a teddy bear that she took nearly everywhere with her.   1

He was just the right size to squeeze into her pocket. Her brother Tristan had fair hair and blue eyes, pale skin and a cheeky smile. He always seemed able to talk her into anything.

She hero worshiped him and believed everything he told her. So when he asked her to get into a large suitcase and said that he was going to close the lid on her she refused. She was proud of herself that she had stood up to him. He soon talked her into it by saying he would get in and she could close the lid on him so she would see it was all right. "Don't lock it and I won't lock it on you," he said and as usual she believed him.

Tristan got into the case and Sukie pushed down the lid but didn't lock it. He climbed out and seemed okay so she got in. He closed the lid then he locked it. She had fallen for it again. She started to scream but in doing so she was using up the air in the case, and her screaming made him panic. He tried to unlock the lid but couldn't, it was stuck.

" I'm going to get Mum," he shouted as he ran from the room.

 "Don't leave me" cried Sukie using up more air but he had already gone. 2

Mum came running in and opened the locks with no trouble and lifted a poor, tearstained, red- faced Sukie and Jeremy Jay out of the case. She gave them both a big cuddle and dried Sukie's eyes.

Mum was furious with Tristan and sent him straight to bed without any tea. Sukie felt it would make no difference, and she needed to take things into her own hands. The next day she took the spider in its box into Tristan's room. She peered around the room, realising that if she put it into his bed it might just crawl away. She settled for putting it into his underwear drawer and smiled to herself at the thought of his screams.

Mum decided to sort through the children's clothes to see what fitted them and what could be given away. She was working her way through Tristan's drawers when she screamed, threw the clothes up in the air, lost her balance, and fell heavily onto the floor. She broke her right arm in the fall and Tristan never even saw the spider. Sukie sighed. It had all gone wrong for her again and she would have to think of something else.

Tristan and the red tricycle

Tristan loved riding his big red tricycle down the hill in front of his dad's shop in the little country village where they lived. Unfortunately, he scared the customers. He had taken the tyres off the tricycle and had added cardboard flaps to the spokes. He cut his knee length school socks from the top to the bottom so they would fly around his feet. He would pedal to the top of the hill on the footpath and then turn round put his feet on the handle bars to freewheel down the hill. As he passed the door of the shop he let out a blood curdling shriek. The metal rims made a loud scraping noise while the cardboard flaps flicked loudly. One old lady in the shop had to sit down as she watched him go by. "Not again!" said his dad rushing out to tell him off. He told Tristan he could ride on the path round the house but not to leave the garden.

Tristan was bored in the garden so he thought of what he could do that would be more exciting. He looked around and found an old metal bath. He tied it to the back of his tricycle and drove round and round the house. The noise it made on the cement path was loud and alerted his mum that he was up to no good. She peered out to see what was going on.   4

She saw Tristan had placed his little sister Sukie and
Jeremy Jay in the tin bath and he was riding full speed
into the wall of the house.

"Oh my goodness you are going to kill that child," said
mum as she ran out and lifted a bumped and bruised
Susie into her arms.

"I was just trying to see how far back we would bounce"
was the only reply he gave her,

Shortly after that Sukie started the local primary school
for the first time. Of course Tristan attended there as
well. She was starting mid- term and so was the only
new girl. She was scared on her first day. The teacher
introduced Sukie to the other children. They were asked
if they knew her so they could buddy up with her for
lunch. Tristan wasn't there because he took packed
lunch with him, but one of their friends, Brian, took her
under his wing.

The next day Mum asked if Sukie wanted a packed lunch
or canteen and she chose canteen. When it got to lunch
time Jeremy Jay told her he was frightened of going in to
the canteen, so they sat on the corridor doorstep. A
teacher came along and asked why she wasn't in the
canteen.

She was worried she would get in trouble so she lied and said "My brother has taken my packed lunch, and he was meant to go to the canteen." Sukie was escorted into the canteen and the teacher laid a meal in front of her. Poor Tristan was caned for stealing her packed lunch. Strangely, Sukie wasn't pleased with herself for what she had done. She thought she would have been happy that Tristan had finally got what was coming to him. Instead she felt guilty and went home and confessed what she had done. She apologised to her brother, and then it was her turn to be sent to bed without tea.

SOMETHING FISHY

Mum was bathing Tristan and Sukie in the bath. It was a large old fashioned white bath with a rim round it. Tristan's favourite trick was to stand beside the taps, squat down, put his hands round his knees and bomb dive into the water. Poor Sukie cowered at the other end and covered her face with her hands in preparation of what was to come. Jeremy Jay sat on the window sill and watched. He hated the bath. Mum had her back to them fetching the large, fluffy towels ready to wrap around them so they could dry themselves. Tristan jumped, and water exploded everywhere, hitting the ceiling. It overflowed onto the floor and soaked mum. It even hit the wall on the other side of the bathroom.

"Tristan, for goodness sake settle down," sighed weary mum.

Tristan grinned cheekily and looked at the water pistol he brought with him with the intention of firing it at his sister. He thought better of it when he heard the tone of Mum's voice. Mum lifted Sukie out of the bath and wrapped her in a big towel, and she wrapped a smaller one round her wet hair. Sukie grabbed Jeremy Jay by the hand and ran off to dry herself and get dressed.   7

Mum took the opportunity to talk to Tristan. She explained that he should be better behaved and be looking after his sister instead of doing things to upset her all the time. She was getting fed up with his mischief. They were only a couple of days into the school summer holidays and she knew it was going to be a long summer with his misbehaving.

Tristan and his friends were going to the river to fish for sticklebacks and Mum told him he had to take Sukie and Jeremy Jay, too. Tristan was annoyed that his little sister was tagging along. None of the others had sisters. Tristan decided to make the outing as awful as possible for Sukie so wouldn't want to come again. His friend Brian's father was taking them all and he sat on a rug close by reading his book while keeping a close eye on them.

They paddled in the river in their Wellington boots trying to catch the tiny fish in jam jars. The fish were very quick and darted away from them. Tristan caught some in his jar, called Sukie over to show her, and then he poured the contents of the jam jar, fish and all, into her Wellington boot. Sukie squealed as the fish swam around inside her boot. Brian's dad came bounding over to see if she was all right.   8

He emptied her boot back into the river, removed her sodden sock and spread it on the rug to dry in the sun. After getting her to dry her foot on the rug she put her wet Wellington boot back on. She ran to join the others. Jeremy Jay kept Brian's dad company on the rug.

By the end of the morning they were all tired and they sat on the rug to eat the sandwiches their mums had provided. Before they ate Brian's dad made them all wash their hands in the river. When they had finished eating they had a short rest before heading for home. They plodded over the fields, and through the barbed wire fences, each holding the wire for each other. Tristan held up the wire for Sukie to climb through but let it down to soon. The wire caught the back of her blouse and her hair got tangled in it. The more she pulled the more tangled she got. Brian's dad tried to comfort Sukie but she was getting hysterical. Eventually Tristan calmed her down. Slowly but surely they freed her, but Brian's dad had to cuts chunks out of her hair with his penknife. Poor Sukie was upset about her hair, so mum made an appointment to take her to the hairdressers the next day to get her hair restyled.

Mum went into the kitchen and noticed that the goldfish aquarium had been filled with sticklebacks and the goldfish were gone. She could hear Tristan on his noisy tricycle and went to ask him if he knew anything about them. She couldn't believe her eyes; Tristan had the goldfish lying on the bottom of his tricycle basket, and informed her he was taking them for a ride.

Mum quickly scooped them up and put them back where they belonged. She then sat Tristan and Sukie down and explained to them that fish cannot live out of water.

Next day Sukie had her hair fixed and new blouse to replace the one that had been torn. She decided it would be a while before she would go on an adventure with the boys again. Tristan smiled.

SUKIE FIGHTS BACK

One of Sukie's favourite toys was her kaleidoscope. She loved the bright coloured pattern when she looked into it. She loved to lie, on a summer's day, on a rug outdoors and look through the kaleidoscope. She would pretend she was watching coloured stars. She could be lost in a world of her own for hours. Of course, she shared it with Jeremy Jay who lay beside her. Tristan made fun of her still playing with Jeremy Jay but he didn't know what she knew. She knew for a fact that Jeremy Jay came alive at night and when he was alone. She had watched Toy Story and knew that often Jeremy was not where she had left him. That was enough proof for her. Tristan could laugh all he liked, but he didn't have a friend like Jeremy Jay.

Since it was summer holidays, Sukie and Jeremy Jay wanted to go star gazing with the kaleidoscope, but she could not find it. She was particular about her things and kept them in special places. Her kaleidoscope was always on the second shelf up at the left hand side in her bedroom. She searched under the shelves, all through her bedroom and finally, dragging Jeremy Jay by the hand, she clumped off downstairs to find Mum.

11

"Someone has been in my room and they have taken my kaleidoscope. I thought maybe Jeremy Jay had borrowed it to go star gazing himself but he said he hadn't. Could you help me find it Mum, please?"

"Okay, Sukie, but I'm sure it is somewhere close by. We will find it." Mum said.

They searched room by room until there was only the lounge left. Mum moved the furniture in case it had rolled underneath. She pushed the settee forward and her eyes widened in disbelief at what she saw. The kaleidoscope was in pieces on the floor. The little coloured jewels were pushed into a pile; a pair of pliers from Tristan's toy toolset and a magnifying glass were beside it. It was completely ruined. When Sukie saw it she burst into tears and so did Jeremy Jay. Mum was furious and tried to comfort her and promised that she would make sure Tristan bought her another one out of his pocket money. If it had been an accident she wouldn't have minded but he had clearly done this on purpose.

Not only did Tristan have to apologise to Sukie and Jeremy Jay he had to buy a new kaleidoscope. He was also grounded from watching television for a week, and he was being sent to bed early. He hated that. He crept downstairs while the others were watching his favourite programme and he tried to watch it through the keyhole and listen to it with his ear against the door. Dad had heard the stairs creaking and opened the door causing Tristan to fall into the room. Now he was in even more trouble and Sukie hadn't had to do a thing. He was doing it all by himself but that didn't mean she and Jeremy Jay wouldn't get their own back. In bed that night they whispered to each other until they had hatched a plan.

Tristan loved playing tricks on people and had once put a plastic spider in the bottom of his little cousin's cup of juice. When the poor child saw it, he threw the cup up in the air and ran screaming from the room. It was just the reaction Tristan had hoped for. He once placed a bar of special soap in the bathroom and when Dad washed his face it was dyed black. Tristan didn't get the reaction he expected that time. Dad chased him round the house until he caught him and then tickled him till he called for mercy.   13

Tristan was always up to tricks. Sukie had thought of the perfect trick to play on him. She went into the trick shop when she was in town with Mum and bought what she needed. Then she quietly crept into Tristan's room, unfolded his duvet and found his pyjamas. She poured itching powder into them and then spread it all over the bed, being careful not to get it on her hands. She put some in his slippers as well, and just for good measure, opened his underwear drawer and poured in the rest. She smiled to herself as she left his room.

After tea, Tristan and Sukie had their baths and got ready for bed. Mum always read Sukie a bedtime story, but Tristan read by himself since he thought he was too big to have mum read to him. Mum had just finished Sukie's story when Tristan called out for her. When Mum went in, he was squirming all over the bed.

"I'm itchy, Mum," he cried, scratching everywhere.

"Hmm. Let me see in case you have a rash," Mum said as she examined him. Although he was red and blotchy from scratching, there was no rash. Mum thought maybe he was allergic to the new washing powder she had used for his pyjamas so she got him a clean pair from his drawer. He put them on and was fine for a few minutes but then the tormenting itches started again. 14

Sukie and Jeremy Jay got up and peered round Tristan's door. Sukie quietly squealed with delight as the sight of her brother jumping from one foot to the other, red in the face, and scratching every part of his body.

"I must have washed those in the same washing powder. Just get into bed without any pyjamas tonight so your body can cool off."Mum said kissing him goodnight. "I will be back in a little while to check on you."

Sukie ran back to bed before Mum could see her. She lay quietly but breathing fast with excitement. Soon there was a loud shriek from Tristan's room. He jumped out of bed, pulled on some underwear and slippers and went downstairs to find Mum. This itch was driving him mad. Mum came back with him and stripped the bed. She put Tristan in the bath again. The water soothed him, but then he noticed the little speckles coming off his skin. He had seen this before. Itching powder. Sukie.

Tristan smiled to himself and realised he was actually proud of his little sister for standing up for herself. On his way back to bed he went into Sukie's room and gave her the thumbs up sign.

"Good one, Sis, you really got me there," He said.

He never told Mum and she always thought it was the washing powder that had caused the problem. As he drifted to sleep in his fresh, clean bed he was thinking of what mischief he could teach Sukie next.

<u>SNOW DAY 1</u>

Tristan had heard it was going to snow tomorrow. He opened the front door; and the freezing wind hit him in the face. He took a pencil and marked the door about four inches off the ground.

"The snow will be up to there in the morning," he told Sukie.

Sukie had her nose up against the window to look out at the dark sky. It seemed to be about eight o'clock at night but it was only three in the afternoon. It was mid-February and Tristan and Sukie had been impatiently waiting for snow so they could finally use the red sleigh they had got for Christmas. She hugged Jeremy Jay closer to her. She had dressed him in the trousers, top and jumper that Mum had made for him. He looked cosy.

"Mum, Jeremy Jay has a bad cold. Do you think it will be okay for him to go out tomorrow if it snows?" she asked.

"No, Sukie, it would probably be better if he stayed tucked up inside, but he could watch you through the window as long as he is well wrapped up," replied Mum.

"Okay, thanks Mum," Sukie said as she fetched the shoe box bed that Jeremy Jay liked to stay in when he was not in bed with her. She kissed him and pulled his little blanket up under his chin, pretended to give him medicine, and then blew his nose. Then she gave him a little kiss and stoked his fur for a few seconds before signalling to mum to stay quiet by putting her finger to her mouth.

Mum nodded and smiled as Sukie went running off to the garage to find Tristan so they could get the sleigh ready for tomorrow. Tomorrow was Saturday so all their friends would be able to come out with them. They gathered together what they would need if the snow was deep. They sorted plastic spades and buckets to put snow balls in, an old hat and scarf, and a large carrot ready for making a snowman. They also got out their warm gloves, scarves, hats and Wellington boots. Then they went to their rooms and got out their snow- suits and warm socks. They had everything ready and now all they had to do was wait.

The rest of the day went slowly, and finally they went to bed with flickers of excitement in their tummies but not before one last glance outside. They were disappointed to see it had not started snowing yet.

Next morning, they were up early, with their two faces stuck up against the window. Yippee! Everything looked magical and white outside, and the snow looked deep. Tristan opened the front door and gasped as the cold air hit him. The snow was exactly at the mark he had pencilled and it was still snowing heavily. Mum insisted they had a warm breakfast before going out. The only other time breakfast had been eaten so quickly was Christmas. They ran upstairs, quickly washed and dressed. Sukie wrapped Jeremy Jay up well and put him on the windowsill so he could look out. He wasn't really keen on the snow anyway so he didn't mind staying inside. After giving him a quick kiss and whispering something to him, she dashed out to the garage to join Tristan getting ready. Some of their friends were already out. Dad had been out for hours clearing away snow from outside the shop. He and some of the neighbours moved it to the sides of the road so it looked like two long white mountains.

Tristan, Sukie and several of the others ran to Brian's house. His driveway rose about ten feet above the road. They climbed the steep steps to his house and were just about to knock on the front door when he appeared around the side of the house.

 The driveway was untouched and brilliant for making snowballs. They all got to work and filled several containers to the brim with snowballs ready for the day. Sukie was the only girl amongst the children but today no one cared.

Tristan had an idea and started throwing snowballs at cars passing by. Soon everyone joined in. The drivers were tooting and shaking their fists at them but that only made them do it more. Two large snowballs hit the windscreen of a car and the driver stopped, got out and shouted at them. He told them how dangerous it was and threatened to report them to their parents. He was getting very annoyed and Sukie was getting scared. She looked around for Tristan and realised that every one of the boys had run off and hidden, and she was all by herself being told off. Sukie started to cry and when the driver saw how upset she was he knew she had learned her lesson and drove off.

20

Suddenly out of nowhere all the boys appeared. They had been hiding behind the hedge. Tristan comforted Sukie, and they decided it was time to do something else. They refilled their snowballs and went off looking for fun somewhere else.As they passed the mountainous peaks of snow outside the shop, another idea came to them.

They divided up and took cover behind the snow mountains on opposite sides of the road. Soon customers came trudging along to the shop, and came under fire from both sides at the same time. This went on until one customer was hit on his way back from the shop and he dropped the eggs he had just bought. He marched quickly back into the shop and fetched out Tristan and Sukie's dad. Dad was very red in the face and angry and shouted at the children to leave his customers alone and to go away and not come back. He couldn't see them behind the snow hills but he could hear them. Tristan and Sukie crouched down so he couldn't see them. Dad took the customer back into the shop and replaced the eggs for him while mumbling crossly under his breath.

The snow started falling heavier and the children decided to go home and warm up. They would meet again later to build snowmen and go sleighing.

Tristan and Sukie trudged back to the house and after pulling off their wet boots and outer clothes, headed straight for the big cushions mum laid out in front of the fire. She had warm clothing waiting for them and hot chocolate and sandwiches. And they were not alone. Jeremy Jay was warming himself by the fire on his very own cushion.

"How did he get there?" laughed Mum. "I told you he is alive," a very smug Sukie replied wrapping her cold hands round the lovely warm mug of hot chocolate.

SNOW DAY 2

After Tristan and Sukie had warmed up and had their lunch, they were ready to get back out in the snow and build a snowman and go sledging. Brian and his brother were already out and had started making a snowman. Tristan and Sukie came and joined in and soon the crowd of children joined them. They decided to make a family of snowmen. They were so busy they didn't notice the snow getting heavier and heavier. They were just outside most of their houses, on the village green, so their parents were able to keep an eye on them from their windows. Sukie looked over to her house and waved at Jeremy Jay who was all wrapped up in his blanket watching them from the windowsill.

The Daddy snowman was getting so big that they had to stand on upturned buckets to reach his face. They put two pieces of coal in for his eyes, the carrot for his nose and the hat and scarf on his face and neck. They used a stick for his mouth. They thought he looked great. The others were still working on the rest of the snowman family so they helped to finish them.   23

The village green looked wonderful covered in snow with six snow people. They also had a snow dog. Their parents and others were looking out the windows and clapping. Passersby stopped to admire them.

The children dragged their sledges along towards the farmer's field called "Daisy Hill". It had the best sledging hill for miles. It was at the bottom of that field that the children went stickleback fishing in the river and in the summer mushroom picking. It also had a huge chestnut tree where the children gathered conkers. In the summer, tents could be seen in the field as it was a safe place for children to camp and be close to home. The farmer's grandson, Robbie, who visited in holidays and weekends often came out to play with them.

 Tristan trudged up to the top of the field dragging the sledge. This was the worst part, the only part he didn't like of playing in the snow. His arms got tired pulling it up the steep hill and he was impatient to have those few minutes of thrill again whizzing down the hill like the wind. Suddenly he had an idea; he ran over to the boys and whispered to them. Sukie and the younger boys were at the bottom of the hill waiting for their turn. The older children Jumped on the sledges, racing each other. They went, faster and faster....whoosh..   24

The younger ones ran over to them, ready for their turn. Tristan told them 'a new rule' had been brought out for younger sisters and brothers. They could only have a ride if they pulled the sledge up the hill after every ride and after they did that three times they could have a ride themselves. Sukie and the others were upset but their big brothers assured them it was true so they had no choice.

Sukie and the others trudged up the hill pulling the sleighs and then ran down to be them up again. Up and down, up and down, up and down until finally it was their turn. Whoosh! Wow! The wind blew in Sukie's face, stinging her eyes and lips but she didn't care. This was fun. Soon she had gotten to the bottom of the hill but had to trudge up again. Up and down, up and down, up and down again and again. After a while the fun was wearing off for the youngest who were exhausted. It didn't seem worth the effort any more. They huddled together whispering.

"Hurry up with our rides!" the older brothers shouted from the top of the hill.

The youngsters found energy from somewhere and started running toward the gate dragging the sledges behind them. Up the snow covered street they plodded to the snow mountains outside Sukie's dads shop. There they put the sledges in the middle of the road (there was no traffic as the snow was so deep) and raced down the hill in front of the shop. That way Sukie knew Dad would keep an eye on them and they would get their turns. The older boys came running round the corner, annoyed, that they had been tricked and started throwing snowballs at them.

Soon a snowball fight began and the snow mountains came in very useful to both sides to hide behind. The fun continued until a blizzard started and they couldn't see across the street. Not wanting the day to end they all grudgingly said goodbye and arranged to meet in the morning.

Mum had the fire stoked, and just as they sat down to get warm the electricity went off. Sukie had lifted Jeremy Jay onto the cushion beside her, because he was frightened, and she held his hand and whispered soothingly to him.

By the light of the fire, Mum lit candles that she had ready just in case. She thought this might happen and had made a big pot of beef stew and a pot of broth. The broth she would use tomorrow but the stew was for tonight.

Dad came in and they sat around the fire with bowls of stew and they each told of their day. The children told excitedly about the sledging, snowballing, and making the snow people. Dad told Mum how there had been naughty children snow balling his customers this morning, and he hoped he never found out who they were or else there might be trouble. As he lifted his fork to his mouth he winked at Tristan and Tristan in turn winked at Sukie. Sukie winked at Jeremy Jay and put her finger to her lips gesturing him to stay quiet.

32078601R00020

Printed in Great Britain
by Amazon